W9-DFR-561

BILLY BATSON AND THE MAGIC of SHAZAM!

STONE ARCH BOOKS
a capstone imprint

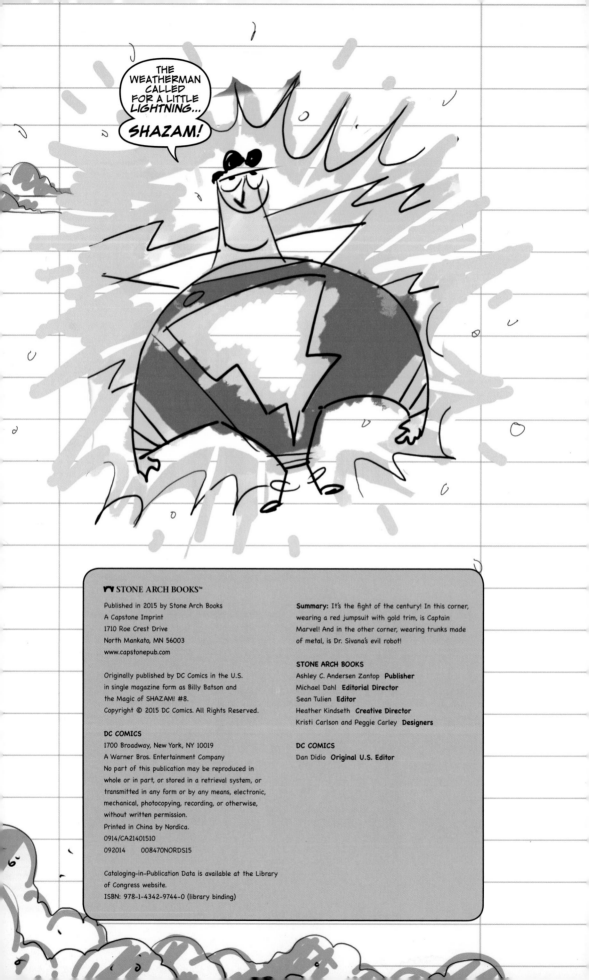

THE WEATHERMAN CALLED FOR A LITTLE LIGHTNING...
SHAZAM!

STONE ARCH BOOKS™

Published in 2015 by Stone Arch Books
A Capstone Imprint
1710 Roe Crest Drive
North Mankato, MN 56003
www.capstonepub.com

Originally published by DC Comics in the U.S.
in single magazine form as Billy Batson and
the Magic of SHAZAM! #8.
Copyright © 2015 DC Comics. All Rights Reserved.

DC COMICS
1700 Broadway, New York, NY 10019
A Warner Bros. Entertainment Company
No part of this publication may be reproduced in
whole or in part, or stored in a retrieval system, or
transmitted in any form or by any means, electronic,
mechanical, photocopying, recording, or otherwise,
without written permission.
Printed in China by Nordica.
0914/CA21401510
092014   008470NORDS15

Cataloging-in-Publication Data is available at the Library
of Congress website.
ISBN: 978-1-4342-9744-0 (library binding)

Summary: It's the fight of the century! In this corner,
wearing a red jumpsuit with gold trim, is Captain
Marvel! And in the other corner, wearing trunks made
of metal, is Dr. Sivana's evil robot!

STONE ARCH BOOKS
Ashley C. Andersen Zantop **Publisher**
Michael Dahl **Editorial Director**
Sean Tulien **Editor**
Heather Kindseth **Creative Director**
Kristi Carlson and Peggie Carley **Designers**

DC COMICS
Dan Didio **Original U.S. Editor**

BILLY BATSON AND THE MAGIC OF SHAZAM!

Come Together!

Art Baltazar & Franco .... writers
Byron Vaughns .... illustrator
Dave Tanguay .... colorist

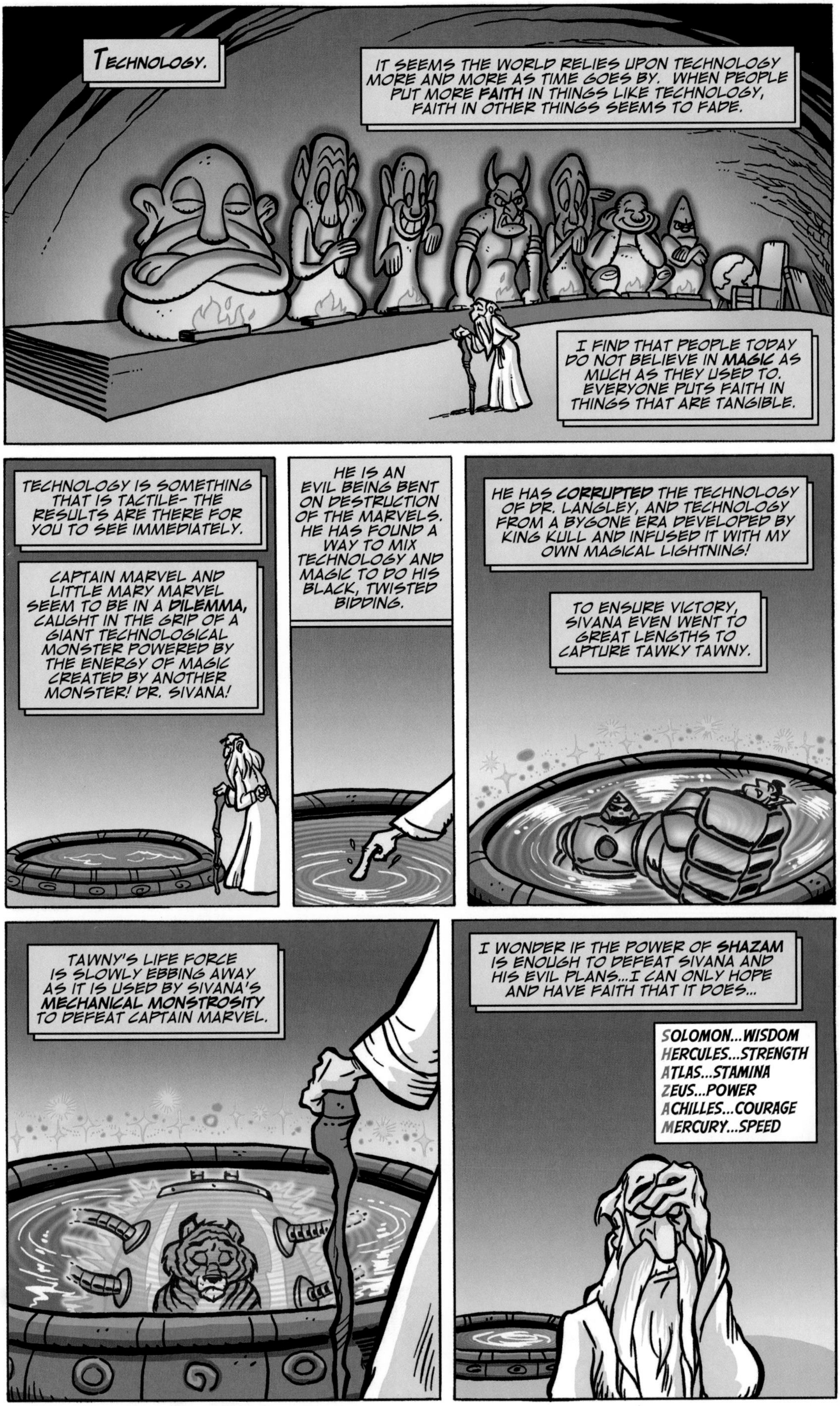
TECHNOLOGY.
IT SEEMS THE WORLD RELIES UPON TECHNOLOGY MORE AND MORE AS TIME GOES BY. WHEN PEOPLE PUT MORE FAITH IN THINGS LIKE TECHNOLOGY, FAITH IN OTHER THINGS SEEMS TO FADE.
I FIND THAT PEOPLE TODAY DO NOT BELIEVE IN MAGIC AS MUCH AS THEY USED TO. EVERYONE PUTS FAITH IN THINGS THAT ARE TANGIBLE.
TECHNOLOGY IS SOMETHING THAT IS TACTILE- THE RESULTS ARE THERE FOR YOU TO SEE IMMEDIATELY.
CAPTAIN MARVEL AND LITTLE MARY MARVEL SEEM TO BE IN A DILEMMA, CAUGHT IN THE GRIP OF A GIANT TECHNOLOGICAL MONSTER POWERED BY THE ENERGY OF MAGIC CREATED BY ANOTHER MONSTER! DR. SIVANA!
HE IS AN EVIL BEING BENT ON DESTRUCTION OF THE MARVELS. HE HAS FOUND A WAY TO MIX TECHNOLOGY AND MAGIC TO DO HIS BLACK, TWISTED BIDDING.
HE HAS CORRUPTED THE TECHNOLOGY OF DR. LANGLEY, AND TECHNOLOGY FROM A BYGONE ERA DEVELOPED BY KING KULL AND INFUSED IT WITH MY OWN MAGICAL LIGHTNING!
TO ENSURE VICTORY, SIVANA EVEN WENT TO GREAT LENGTHS TO CAPTURE TAWKY TAWNY.
TAWNY'S LIFE FORCE IS SLOWLY EBBING AWAY AS IT IS USED BY SIVANA'S MECHANICAL MONSTROSITY TO DEFEAT CAPTAIN MARVEL.
I WONDER IF THE POWER OF SHAZAM IS ENOUGH TO DEFEAT SIVANA AND HIS EVIL PLANS...I CAN ONLY HOPE AND HAVE FAITH THAT IT DOES...
SOLOMON...WISDOM
HERCULES...STRENGTH
ATLAS...STAMINA
ZEUS...POWER
ACHILLES...COURAGE
MERCURY...SPEED

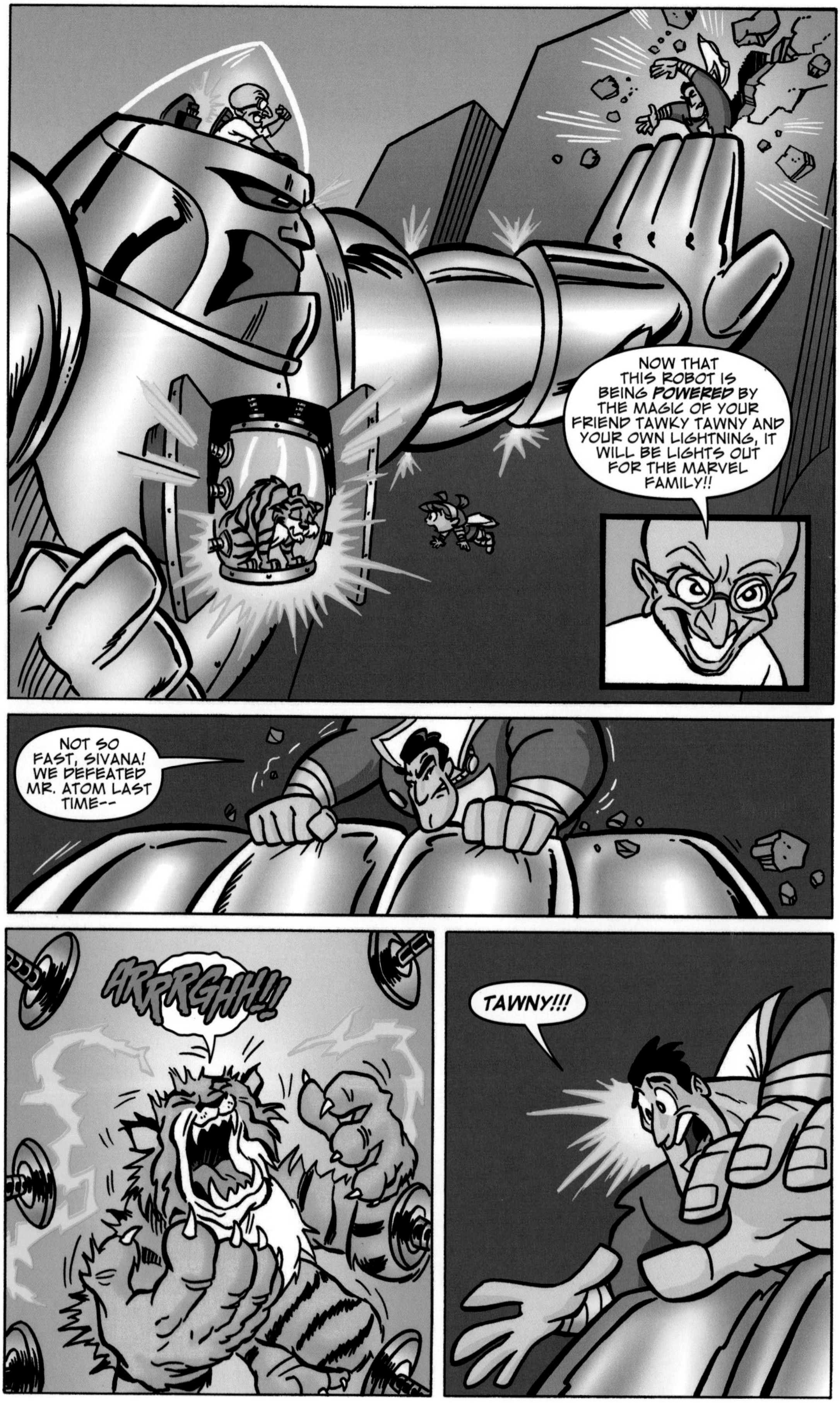

NOW THAT THIS ROBOT IS BEING POWERED BY THE MAGIC OF YOUR FRIEND TAWKY TAWNY AND YOUR OWN LIGHTNING, IT WILL BE LIGHTS OUT FOR THE MARVEL FAMILY!!
NOT SO FAST, SIVANA! WE DEFEATED MR. ATOM LAST TIME--
ARRRGHH!!!
TAWNY!!!

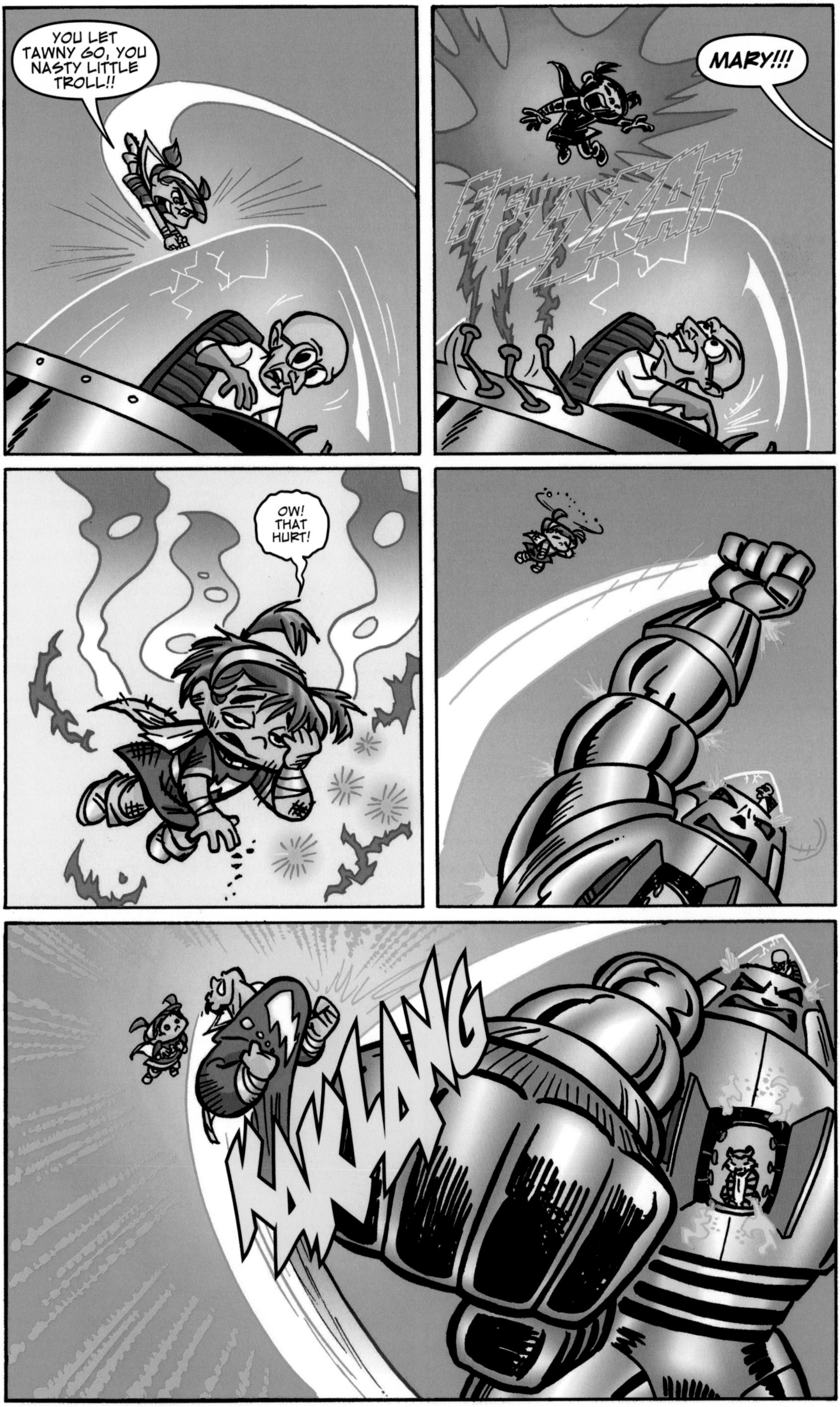

YOU LET TAWNY GO, YOU NASTY LITTLE TROLL!!
MARY!!!
OW! THAT HURT!
KAKLANG

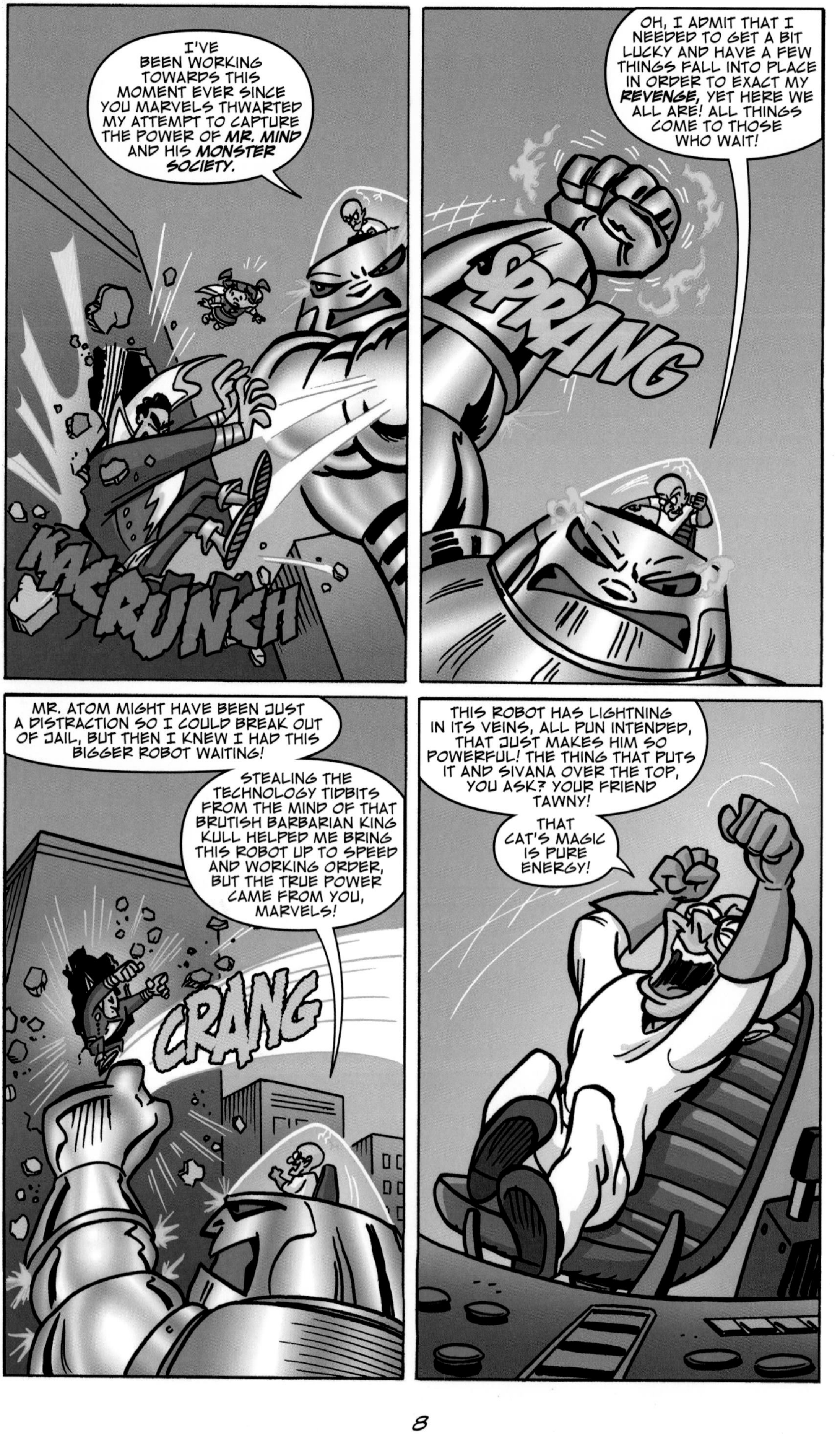
I'VE BEEN WORKING TOWARDS THIS MOMENT EVER SINCE YOU MARVELS THWARTED MY ATTEMPT TO CAPTURE THE POWER OF MR. MIND AND HIS MONSTER SOCIETY.
KRACRUNCH
OH, I ADMIT THAT I NEEDED TO GET A BIT LUCKY AND HAVE A FEW THINGS FALL INTO PLACE IN ORDER TO EXACT MY REVENGE, YET HERE WE ALL ARE! ALL THINGS COME TO THOSE WHO WAIT!
SPRANG
MR. ATOM MIGHT HAVE BEEN JUST A DISTRACTION SO I COULD BREAK OUT OF JAIL, BUT THEN I KNEW I HAD THIS BIGGER ROBOT WAITING!
STEALING THE TECHNOLOGY TIDBITS FROM THE MIND OF THAT BRUTISH BARBARIAN KING KULL HELPED ME BRING THIS ROBOT UP TO SPEED AND WORKING ORDER, BUT THE TRUE POWER CAME FROM YOU, MARVELS!
CRANG
THIS ROBOT HAS LIGHTNING IN ITS VEINS, ALL PUN INTENDED, THAT JUST MAKES HIM SO POWERFUL! THE THING THAT PUTS IT AND SIVANA OVER THE TOP, YOU ASK? YOUR FRIEND TAWNY!
THAT CAT'S MAGIC IS PURE ENERGY!

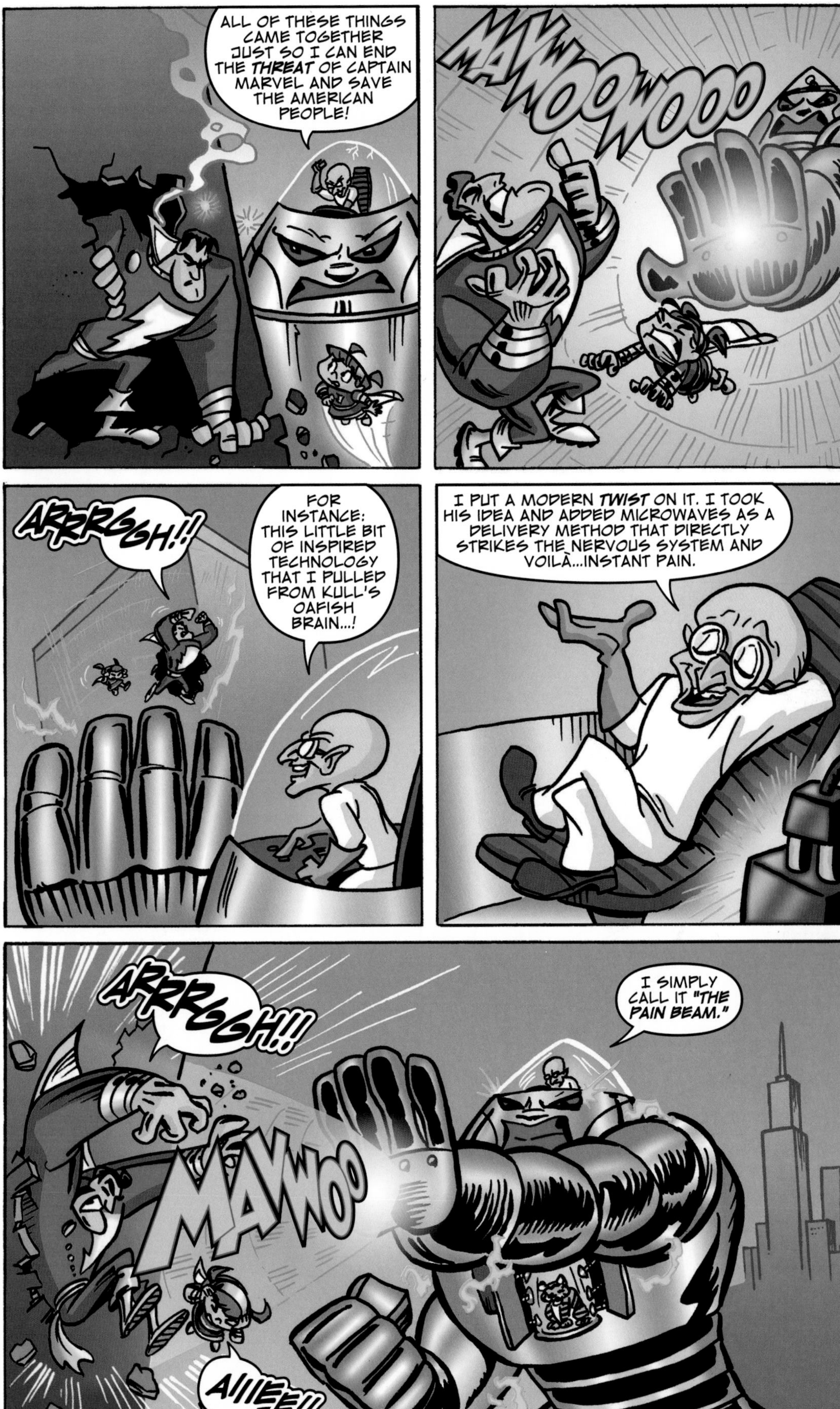
ALL OF THESE THINGS CAME TOGETHER JUST SO I CAN END THE THREAT OF CAPTAIN MARVEL AND SAVE THE AMERICAN PEOPLE!
MAWOOOWOOO
ARRRGGH!!
FOR INSTANCE: THIS LITTLE BIT OF INSPIRED TECHNOLOGY THAT I PULLED FROM KULL'S OAFISH BRAIN...!
I PUT A MODERN TWIST ON IT. I TOOK HIS IDEA AND ADDED MICROWAVES AS A DELIVERY METHOD THAT DIRECTLY STRIKES THE NERVOUS SYSTEM AND VOILÀ...INSTANT PAIN.
ARRRGGH!!
I SIMPLY CALL IT "THE PAIN BEAM."
MAWOO
AIIIEE!!

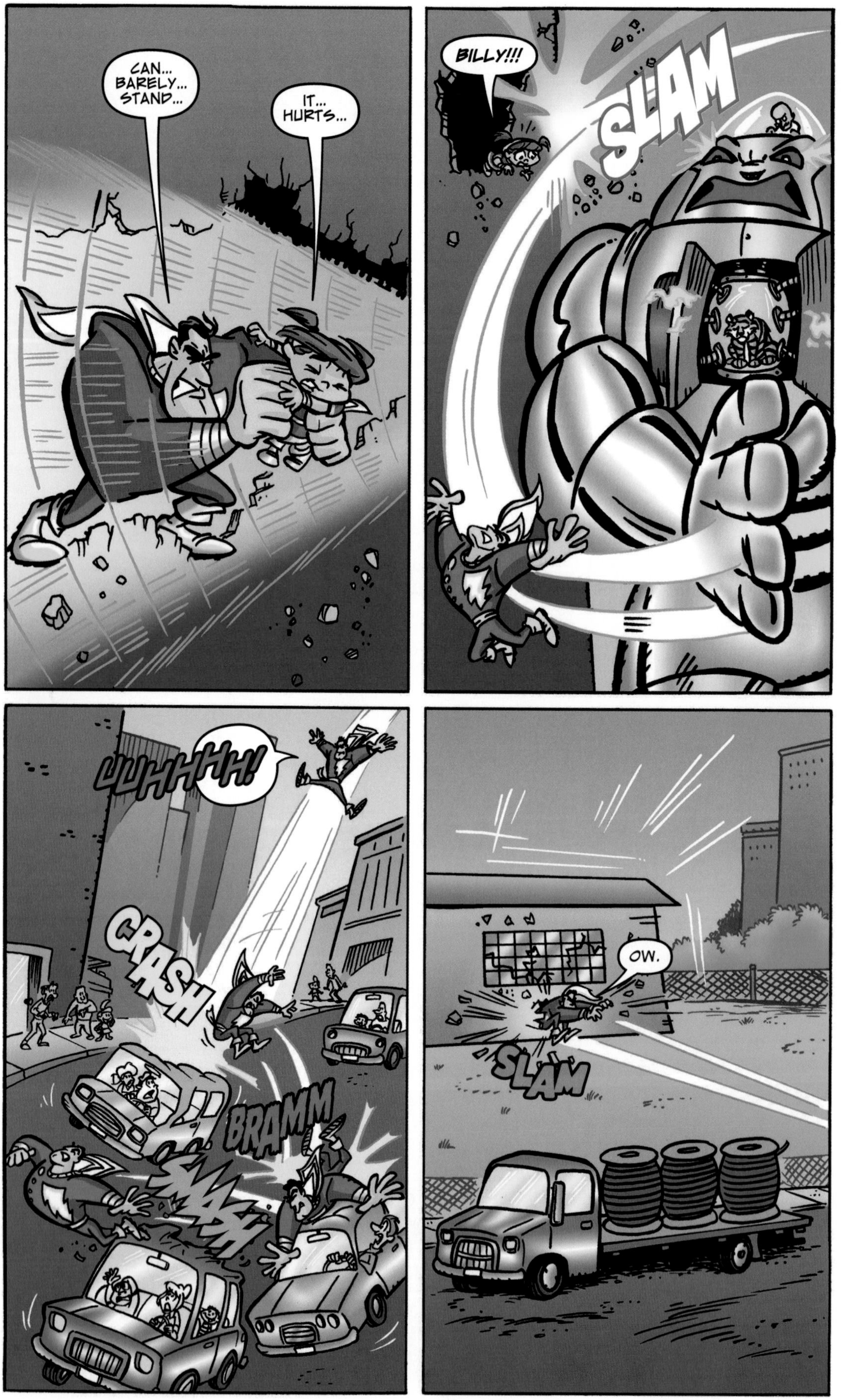
CAN... BARELY... STAND...
IT... HURTS...
BILLY!!!
SLAM
UUHHHHH!
CRASH
BRAMM
SMASH
OW.
SLAM

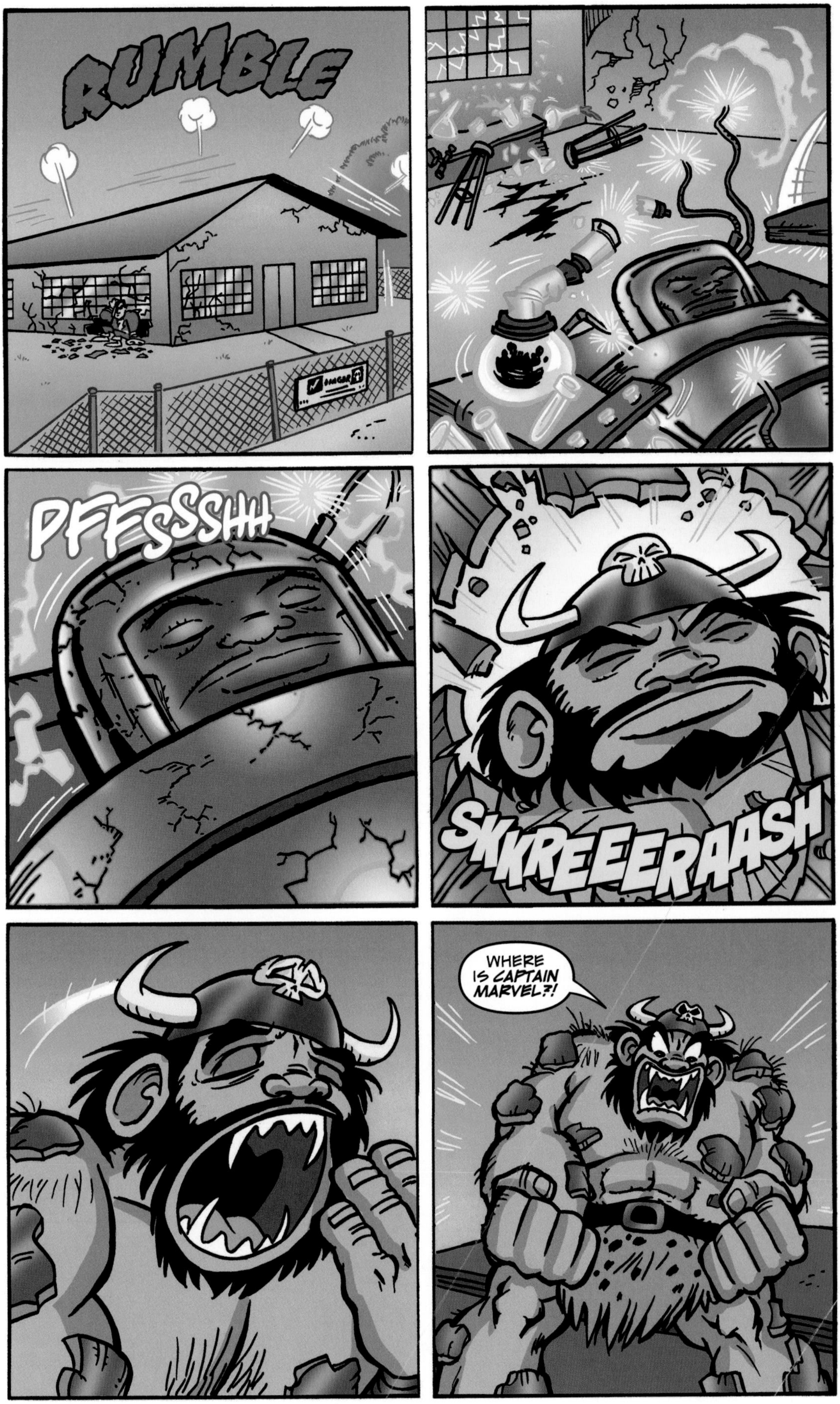
RUMBLE
PFFSSSHH
SKKREEERAASH
WHERE IS CAPTAIN MARVEL?!

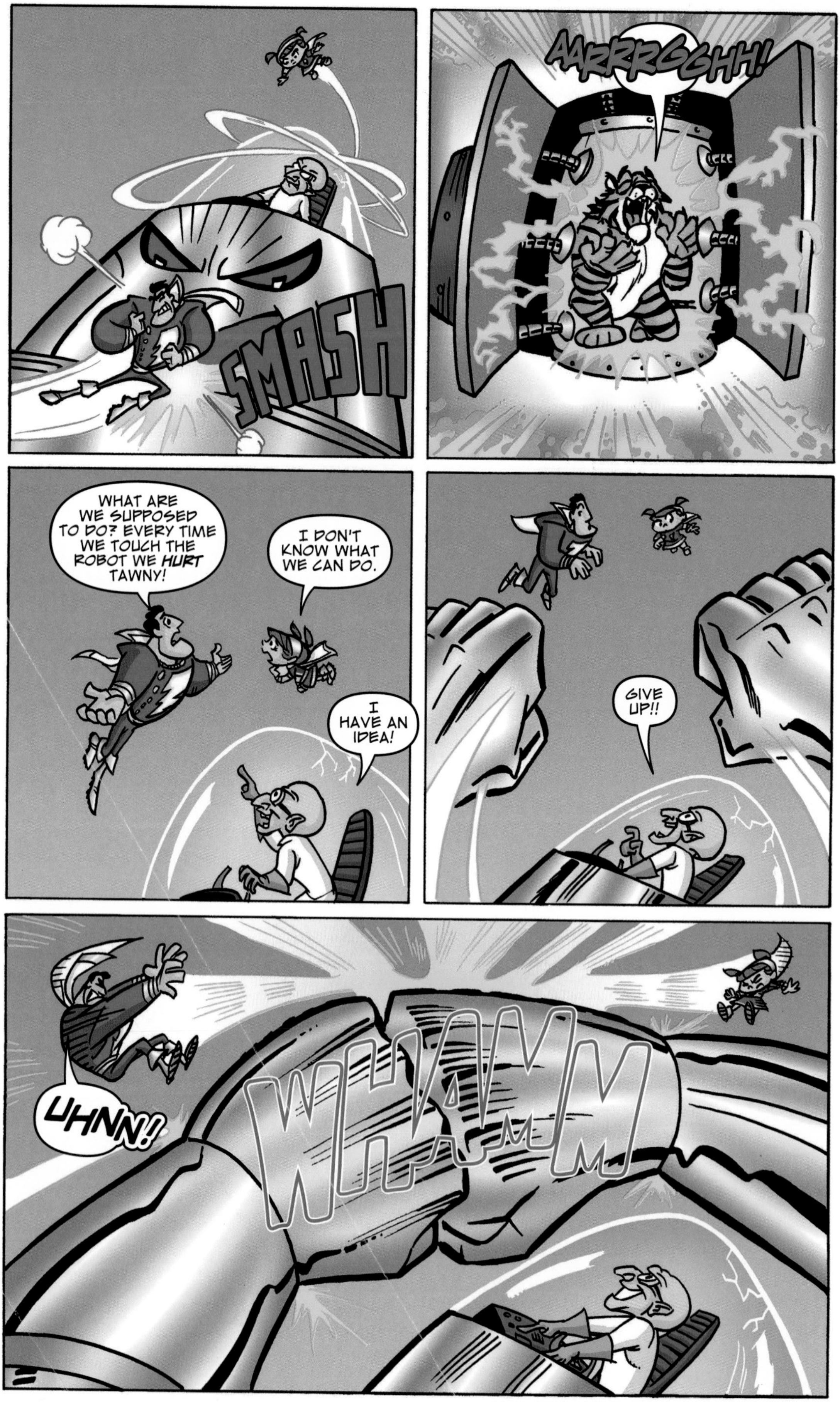
SMASH
AARRRGGHH!
WHAT ARE WE SUPPOSED TO DO? EVERY TIME WE TOUCH THE ROBOT WE HURT TAWNY!
I DON'T KNOW WHAT WE CAN DO.
I HAVE AN IDEA!
GIVE UP!!
UHNN!
WHAMM

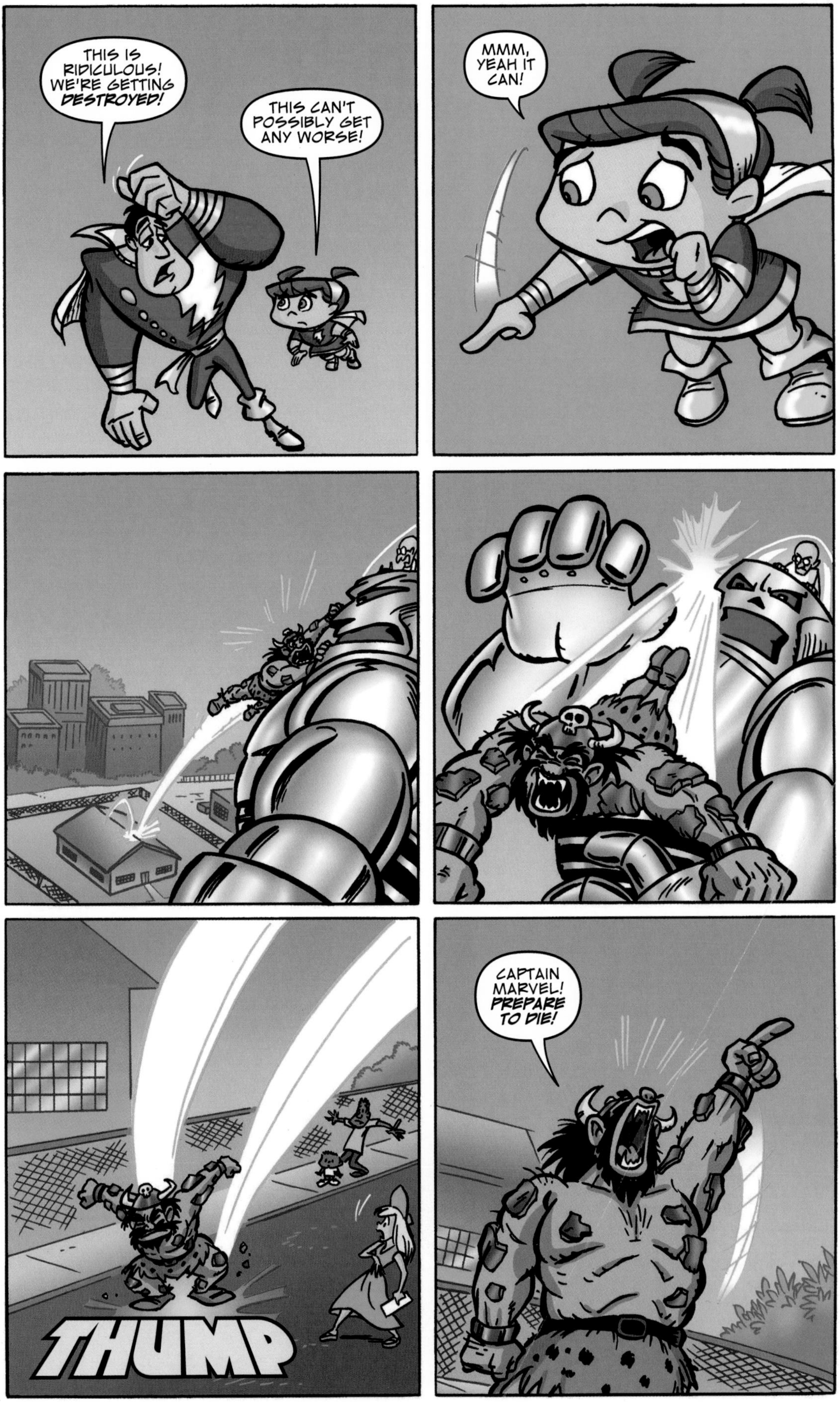
THIS IS RIDICULOUS! WE'RE GETTING **DESTROYED!**
THIS CAN'T POSSIBLY GET ANY WORSE!
MMM, YEAH IT CAN!
THUMP
CAPTAIN MARVEL! **PREPARE TO DIE!**

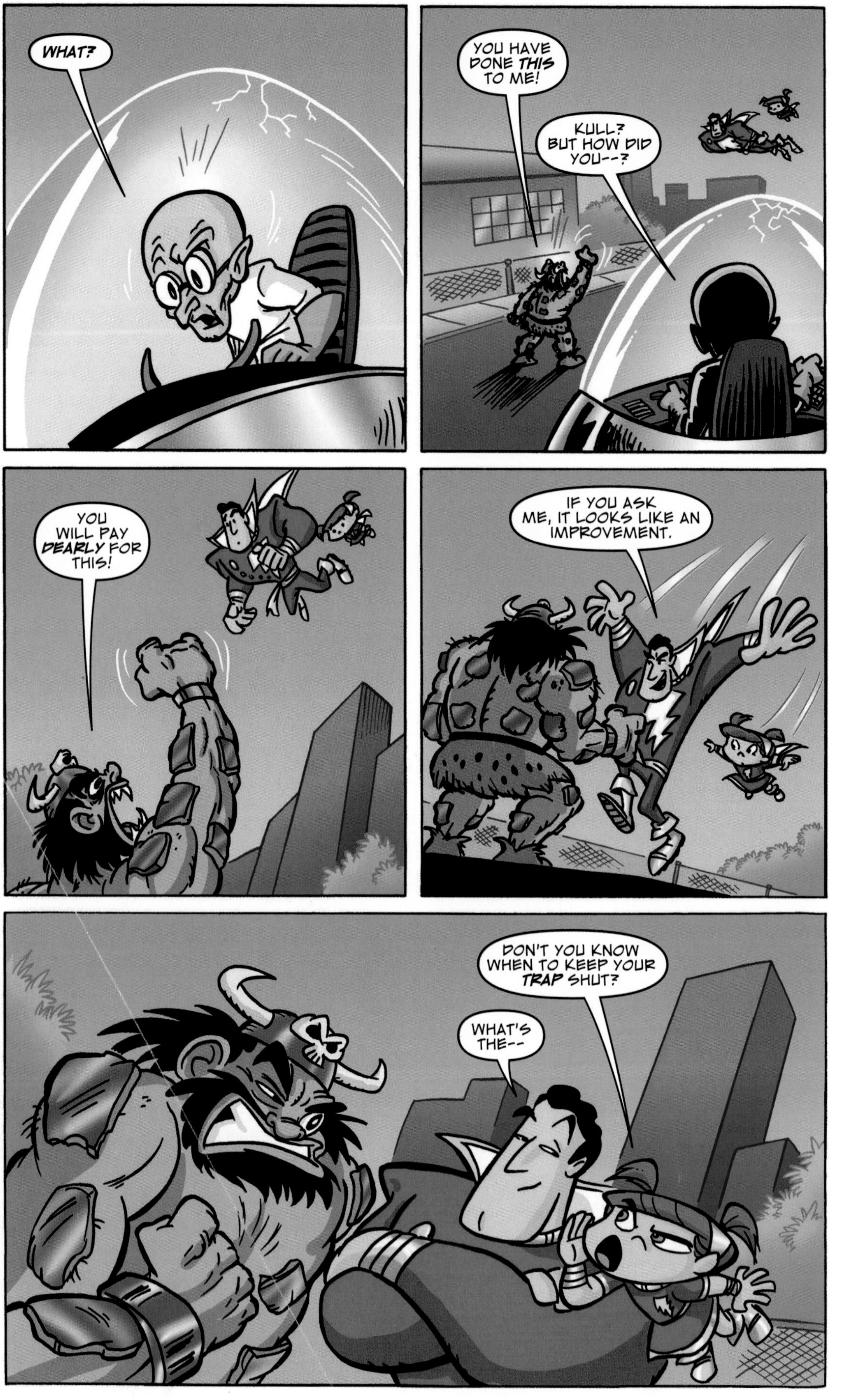
WHAT?
YOU HAVE DONE THIS TO ME!
KULL? BUT HOW DID YOU--?
YOU WILL PAY DEARLY FOR THIS!
IF YOU ASK ME, IT LOOKS LIKE AN IMPROVEMENT.
WHAT'S THE--
DON'T YOU KNOW WHEN TO KEEP YOUR TRAP SHUT?

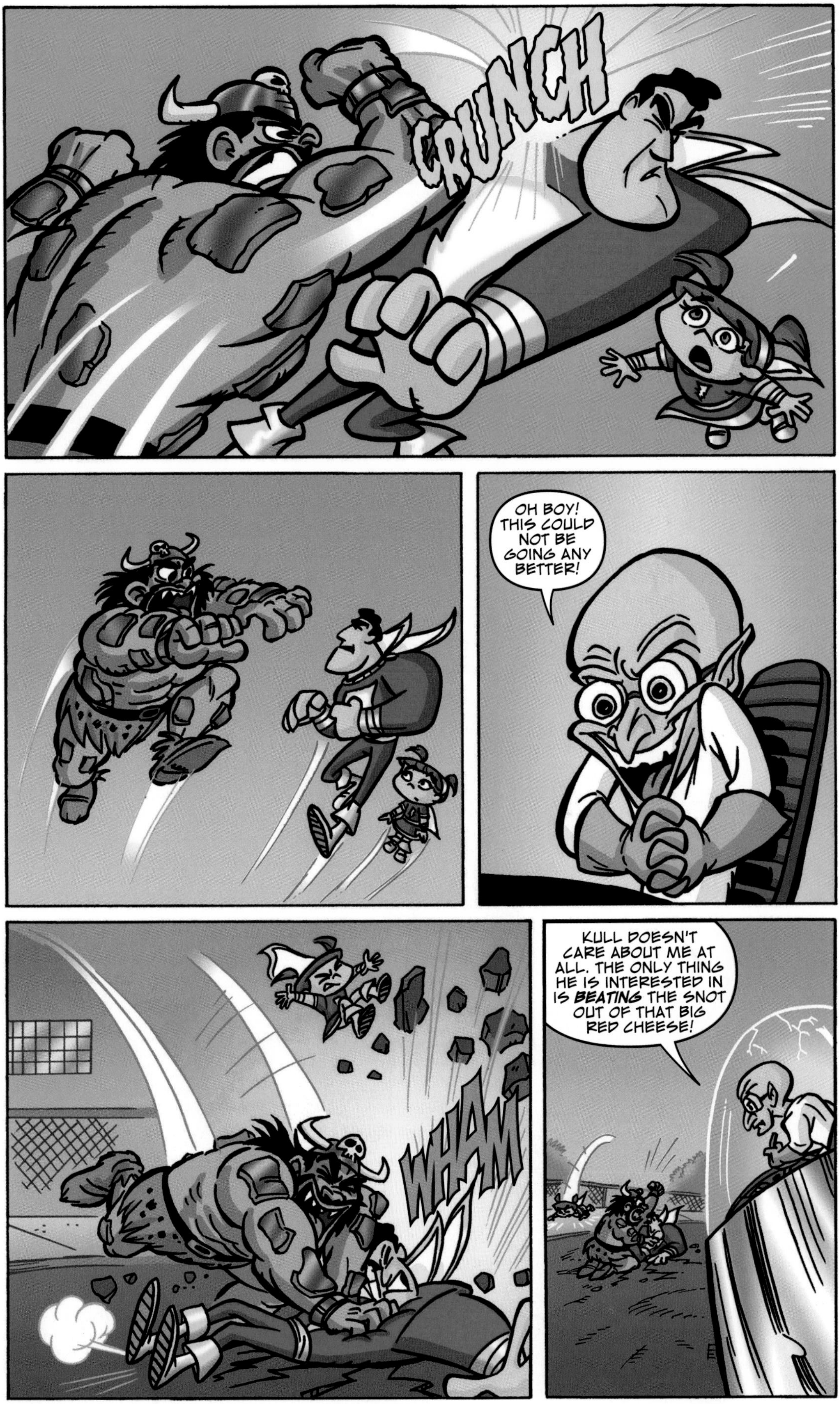
CRUNCH
OH BOY! THIS COULD NOT BE GOING ANY BETTER!
WHAM
KULL DOESN'T CARE ABOUT ME AT ALL. THE ONLY THING HE IS INTERESTED IN IS BEATING THE SNOT OUT OF THAT BIG RED CHEESE!

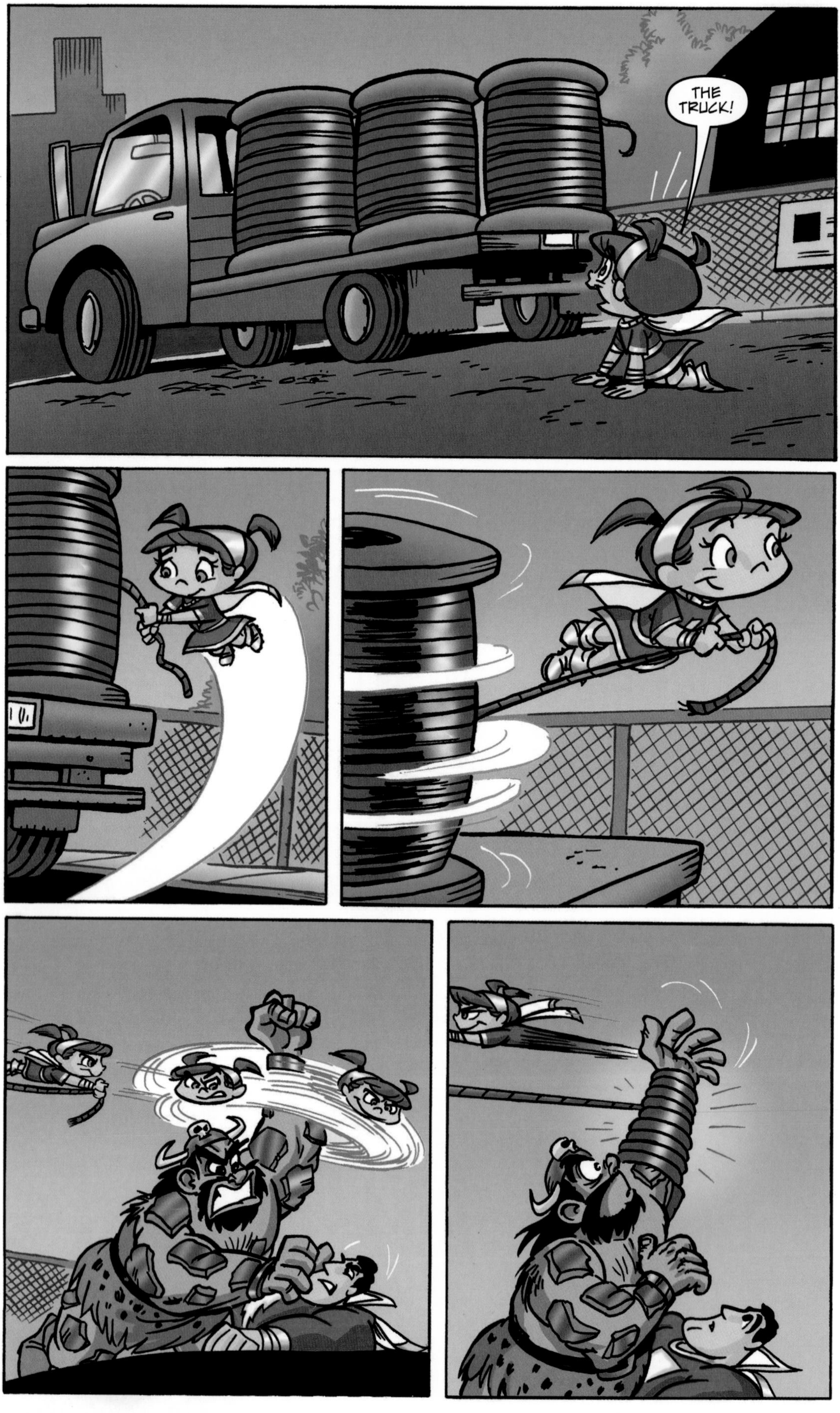
THE TRUCK!

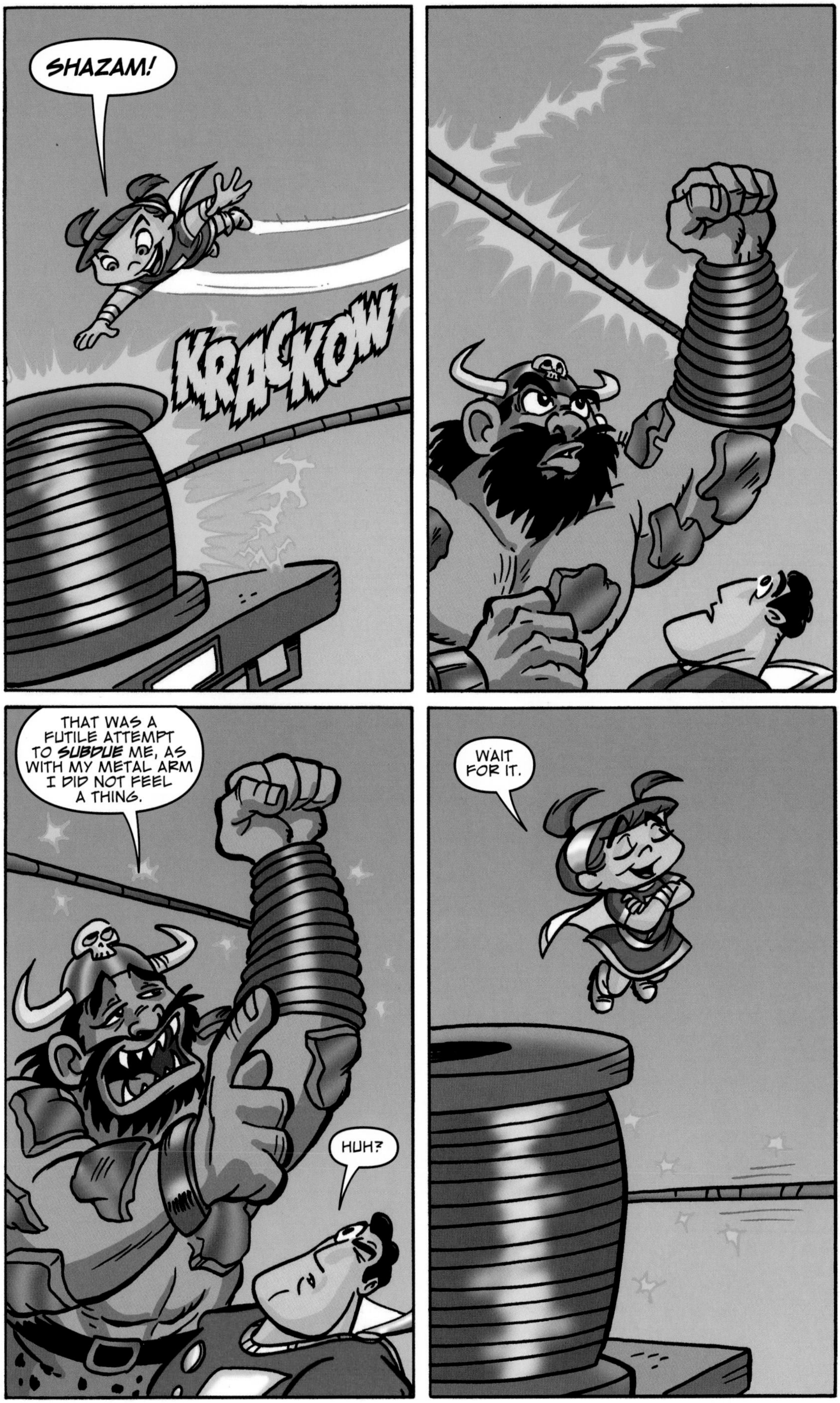
SHAZAM!
KRACKOW
THAT WAS A FUTILE ATTEMPT TO SUBDUE ME, AS WITH MY METAL ARM I DID NOT FEEL A THING.
HUH?
WAIT FOR IT.

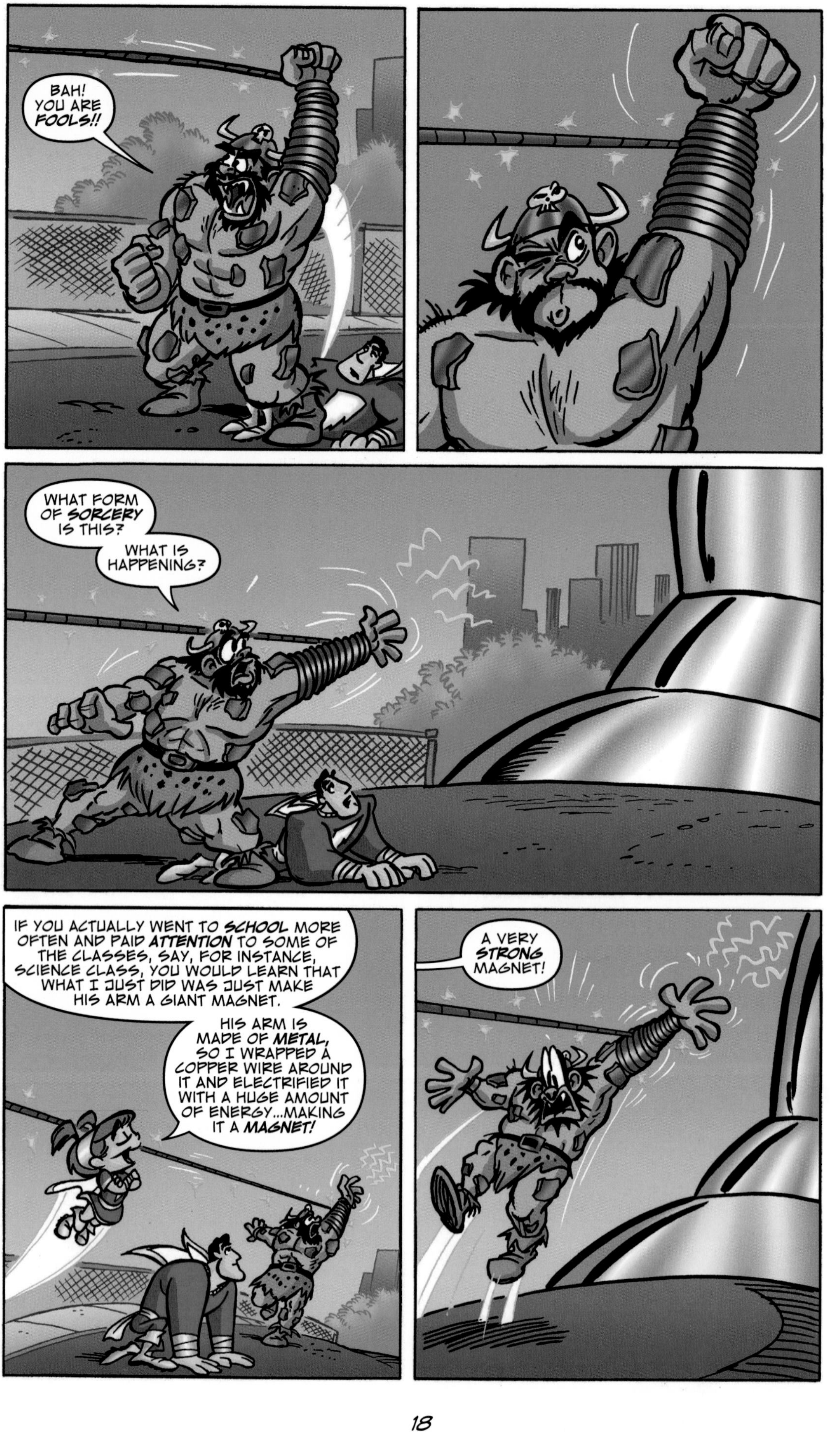
BAH! YOU ARE FOOLS!!
WHAT FORM OF SORCERY IS THIS?
WHAT IS HAPPENING?
IF YOU ACTUALLY WENT TO SCHOOL MORE OFTEN AND PAID ATTENTION TO SOME OF THE CLASSES, SAY, FOR INSTANCE, SCIENCE CLASS, YOU WOULD LEARN THAT WHAT I JUST DID WAS JUST MAKE HIS ARM A GIANT MAGNET.
HIS ARM IS MADE OF METAL, SO I WRAPPED A COPPER WIRE AROUND IT AND ELECTRIFIED IT WITH A HUGE AMOUNT OF ENERGY...MAKING IT A MAGNET!
A VERY STRONG MAGNET!

IF YOU'RE GOING TO BE A SUPERHERO, YOU NEED TO BE **SMART** AS WELL AS STRONG!

THAT'S COOL!

WHAT?

KER-CHUNK

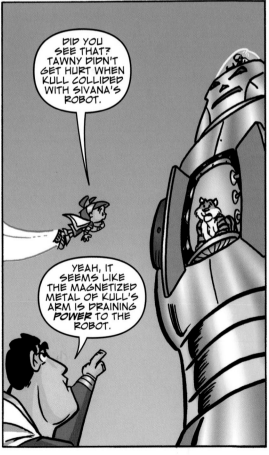

DID YOU SEE THAT? TAWNY DIDN'T GET HURT WHEN KULL COLLIDED WITH SIVANA'S ROBOT.

YEAH, IT SEEMS LIKE THE MAGNETIZED METAL OF KULL'S ARM IS DRAINING **POWER** TO THE ROBOT.

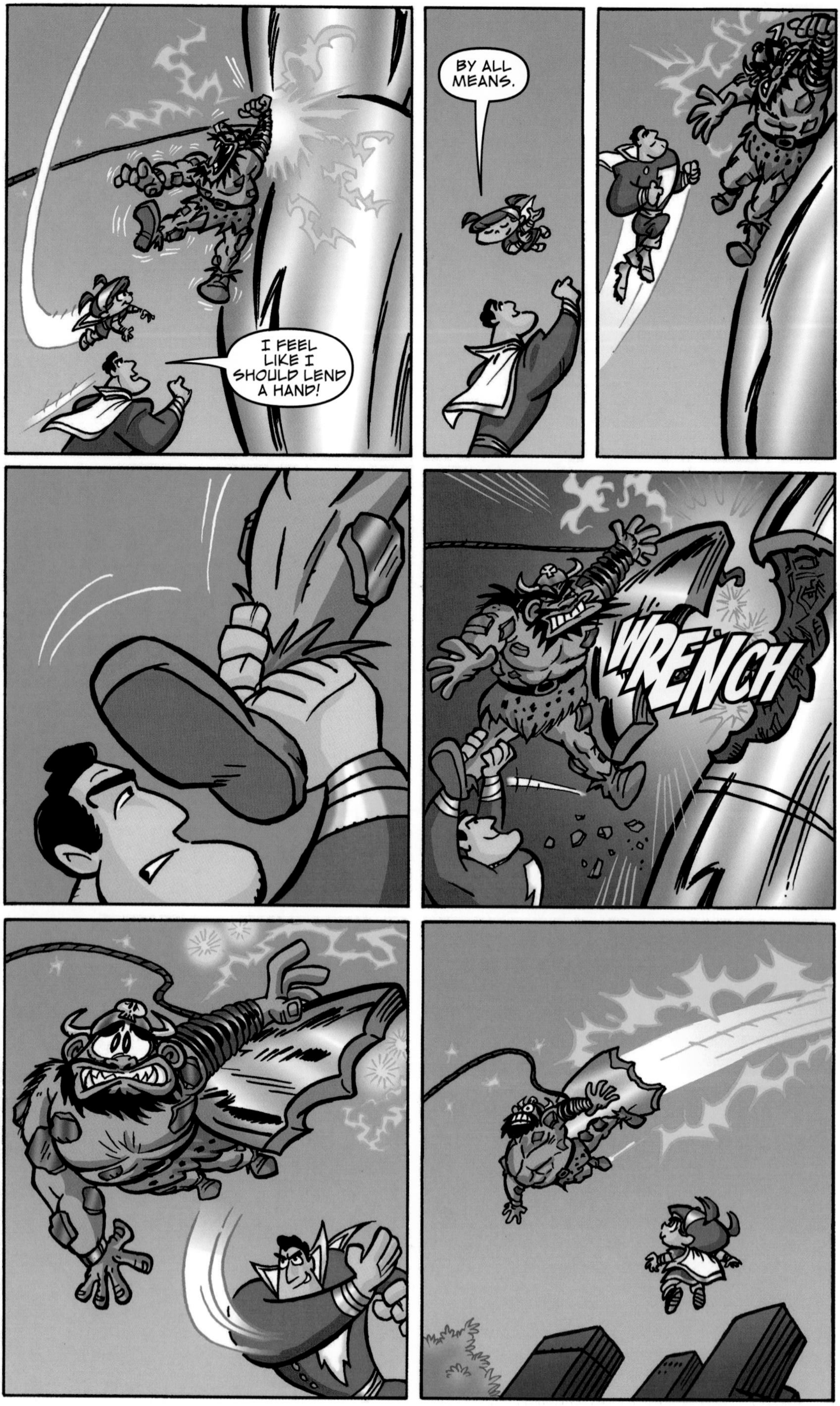
I FEEL LIKE I SHOULD LEND A HAND!
BY ALL MEANS.
WRENCH

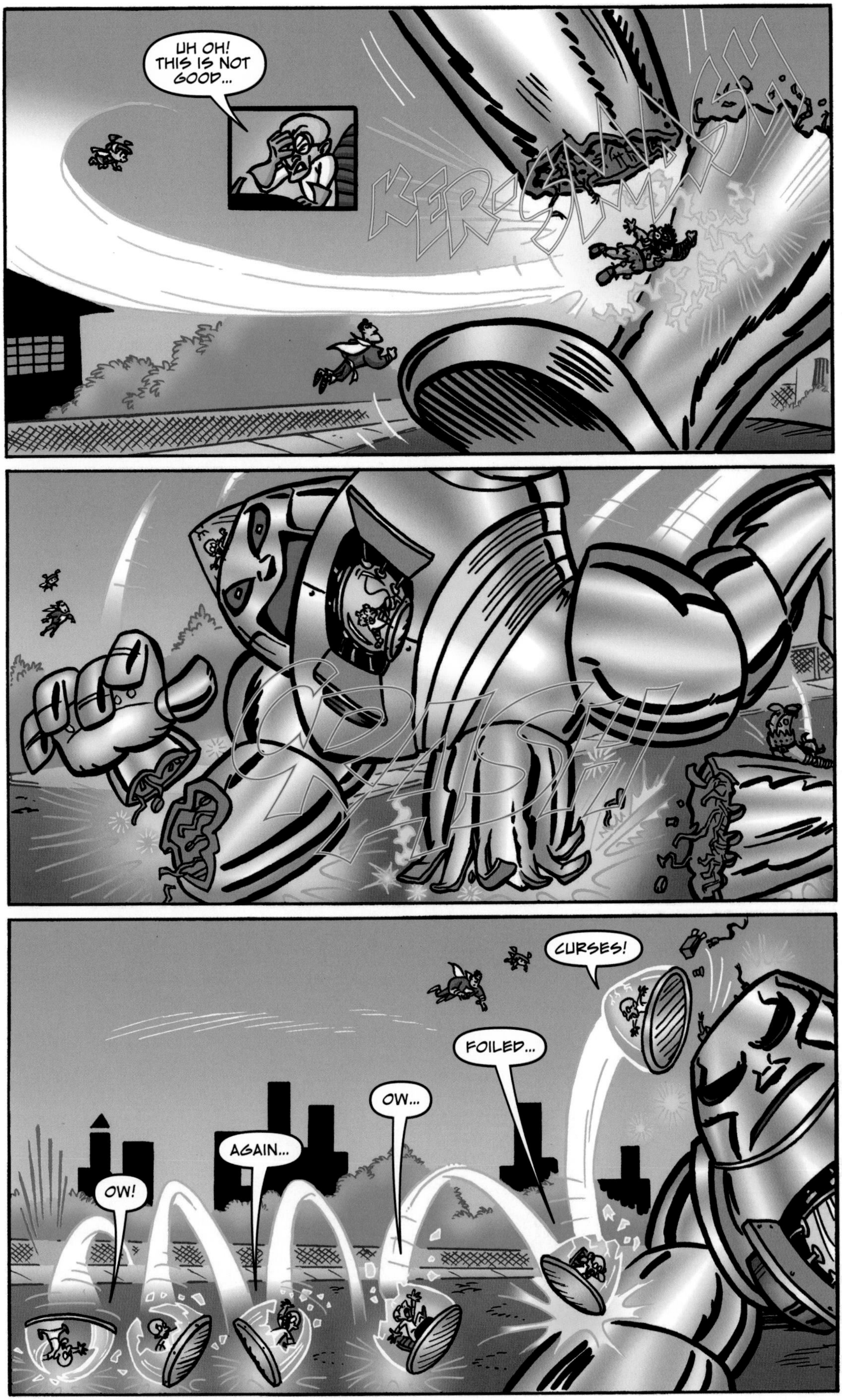
UH OH!
THIS IS NOT
GOOD...
KER-SMASH!
CRASH!
CURSES!
FOILED...
OW...
AGAIN...
OW!

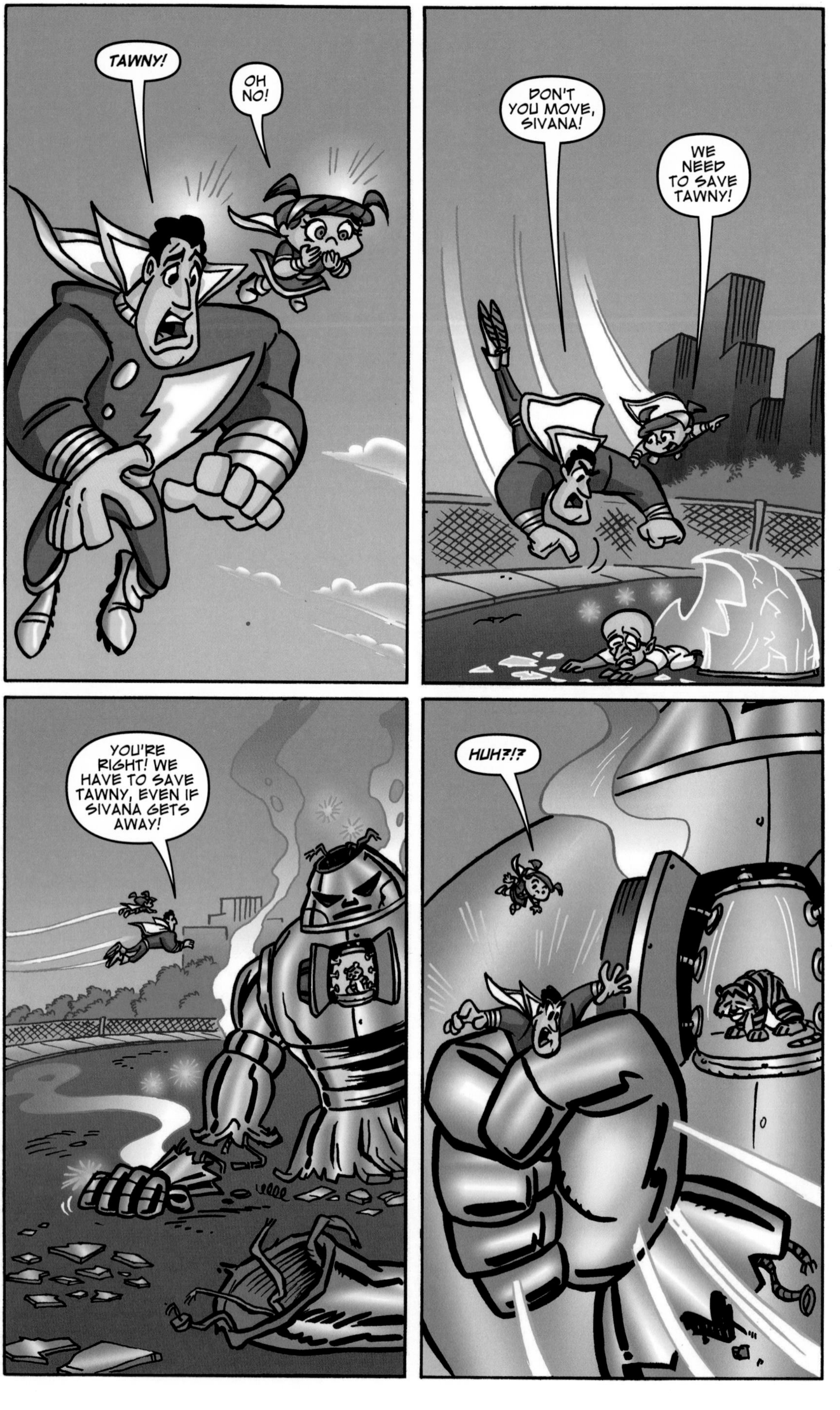
TAWNY!
OH NO!
DON'T YOU MOVE, SIVANA!
WE NEED TO SAVE TAWNY!
YOU'RE RIGHT! WE HAVE TO SAVE TAWNY, EVEN IF SIVANA GETS AWAY!
HUH?!?

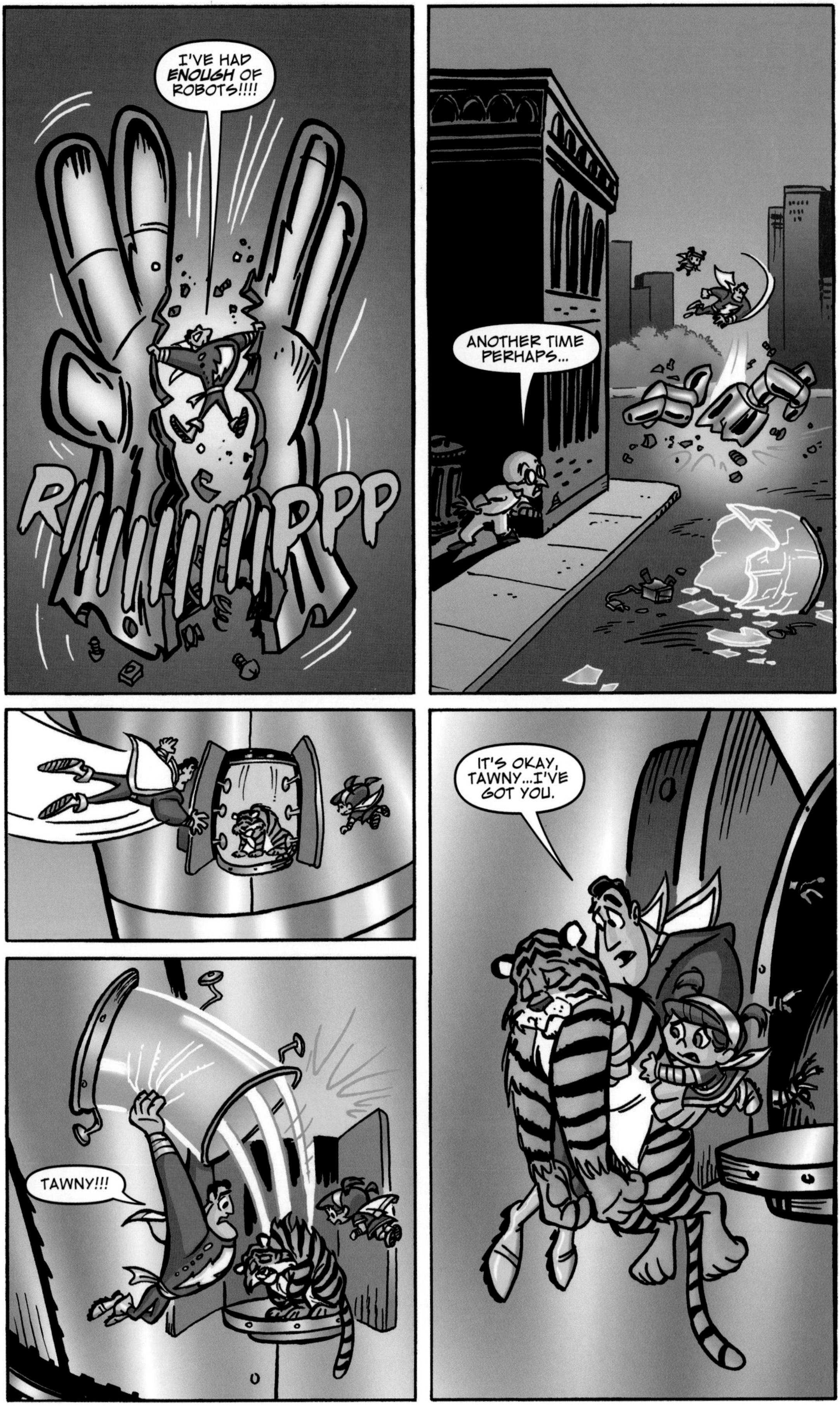
I'VE HAD ENOUGH OF ROBOTS!!!!
RIIIIIIIIIPPP
ANOTHER TIME PERHAPS...
TAWNY!!!
IT'S OKAY, TAWNY...I'VE GOT YOU.

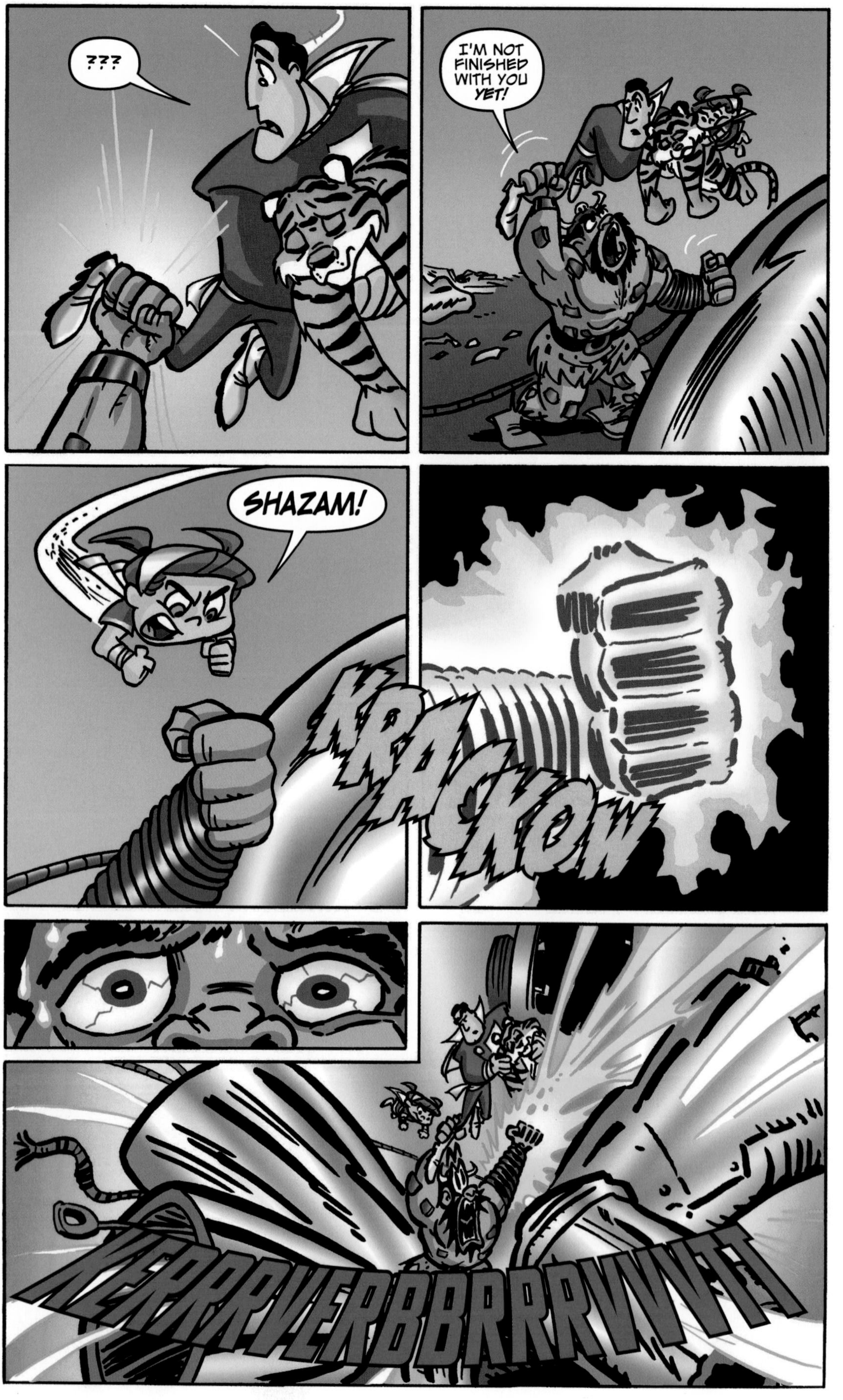
???
I'M NOT FINISHED WITH YOU *YET!*
SHAZAM!
KRACKOW
NERRRVERBBRRRRVVVVT!

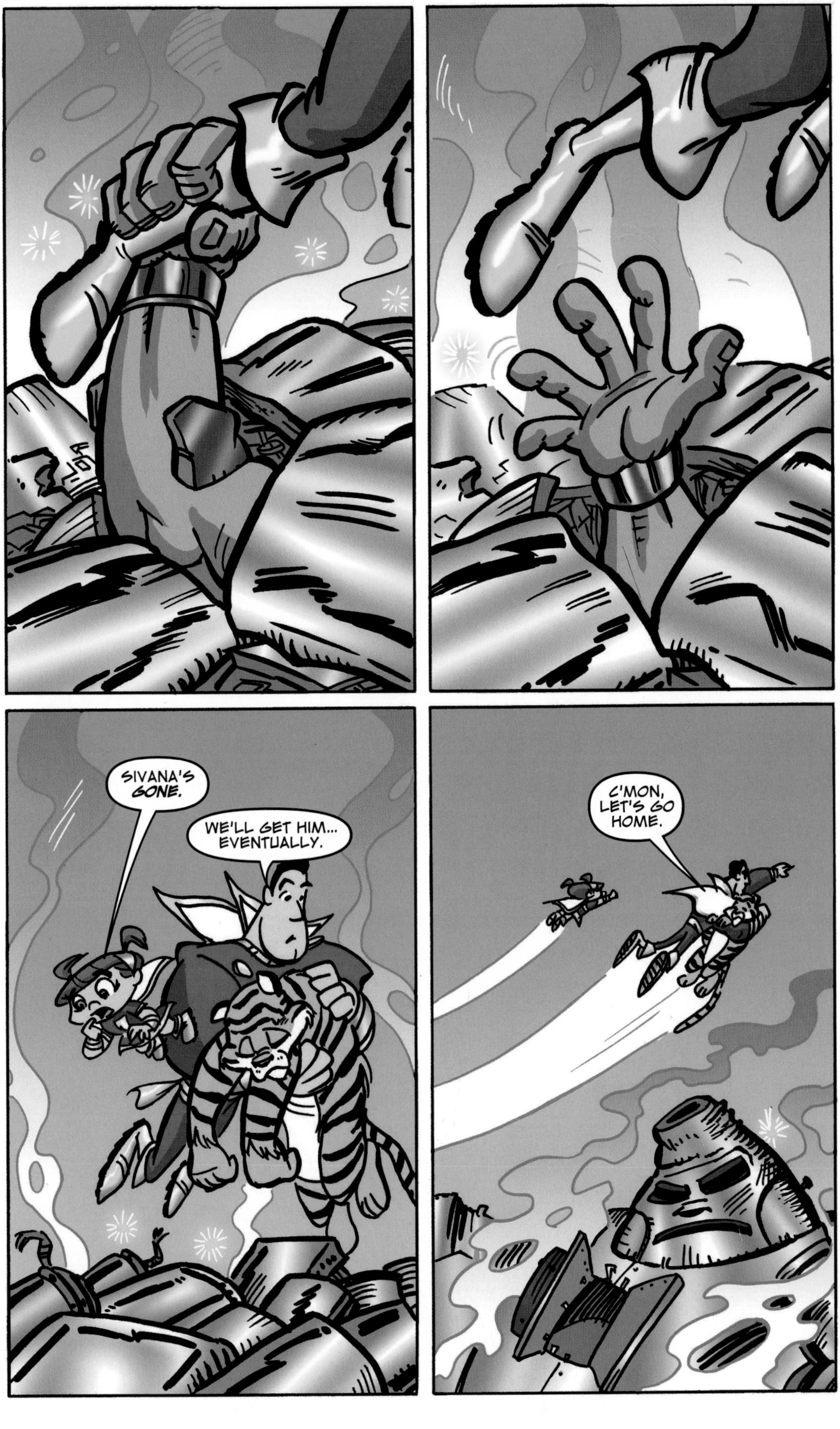
SIVANA'S GONE.
WE'LL GET HIM... EVENTUALLY.
C'MON, LET'S GO HOME.

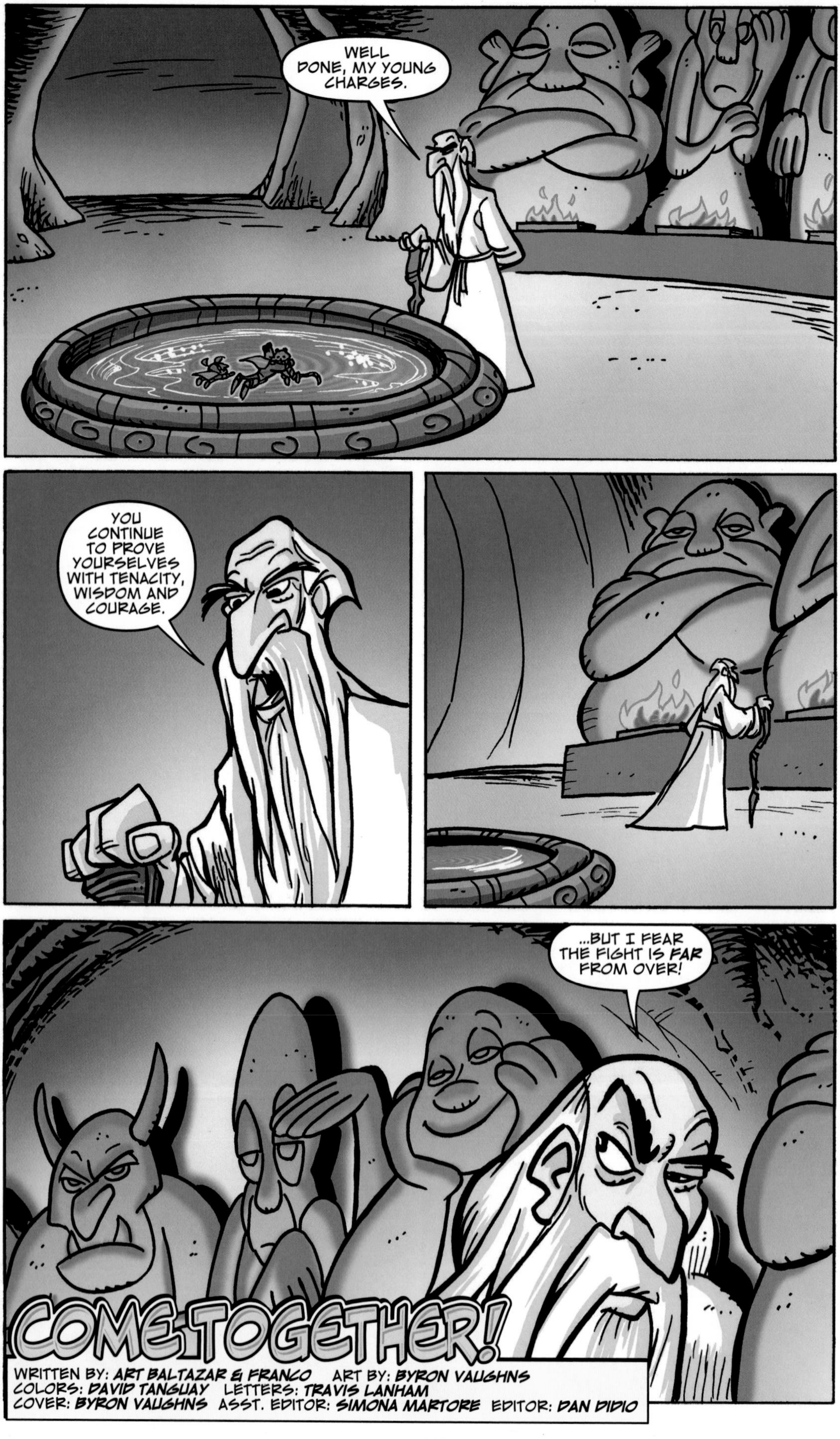

WELL DONE, MY YOUNG CHARGES.
YOU CONTINUE TO PROVE YOURSELVES WITH TENACITY, WISDOM AND COURAGE.
...BUT I FEAR THE FIGHT IS FAR FROM OVER!
COME TOGETHER!
WRITTEN BY: ART BALTAZAR & FRANCO ART BY: BYRON VAUGHNS
COLORS: DAVID TANGUAY LETTERS: TRAVIS LANHAM
COVER: BYRON VAUGHNS ASST. EDITOR: SIMONA MARTORE EDITOR: DAN DIDIO

CREATORS

ART BALTAZAR - CO-WRITER

Born in Chicago, **Art Baltazar** has been cartooning ever since he can recall. Art has worked on award-winning series like Tiny Titans and Superman Family Adventures. He lives outside of Chicago with his wife, Rose, and children Sonny, Gordon, and Audrey.

FRANCO - CO-WRITER

Franco Aureliani has been drawing comics ever since he could hold a crayon. He resides in upstate New York with his wife, Ivette, and son, Nicolas, and spends most of his days working on comics. Franco has worked on Superman Family Adventures and Tiny Titans, and he also teaches high school art.

GLOSSARY

bidding (BID-ing)--if you do something at someone's bidding, you do what someone has ordered you to do

charges (CHARJ-iz)--people (such as children) that another person must guard or take care of

corrupted (kuh-RUHP-tid)--changed something or someone so that it is less pure, honest, or valuable

dilemma (di-LEM-uh)--a situation in which you have to make a difficult choice

faith (FAYTH)--strong belief or trust in someone or something without proof

futile (FYOO-tuhl)--having no result or effect. Pointless or useless.

infused (in-FYOOZD)--filled or mixed with something (like a quality or substance)

marvel (MAHR-vuhl)--something that causes wonder, admiration, or astonishment

monstrosity (mon-STRAHSS-i-tee)--something that is very large and ugly

sorcery (SOHR-suh-ree)--the use of magical powers that are obtained through evil spirits

tangible (TAN-juh-buhl)--able to be touched or felt

tenacity (tuh-NASS-i-tee)--if you have tenacity, you are very determined to do something

thwarted (THWAHR-tid)--stopped someone from doing something

VISUAL QUESTIONS & PROMPTS

1. What do the wispy shapes and colorful bursts around Mary mean? Explain your answer.

2. What is the source of the robot's power? How does it work? Why is this a problem for Mary and Billy?

3. What is happening here? How did it happen? Reread pages 18-19 if you aren't sure.

4. What is the purpose of that little pool in the cave? How do you know?

READ THEM ALL!

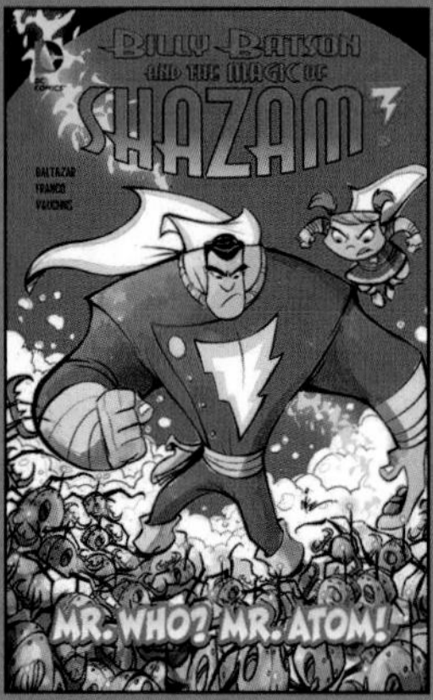
BILLY BATSON AND THE MAGIC OF SHAZAM!
BALTAZAR FRANCO VAUGHNS
MR. WHO?-MR. ATOM!

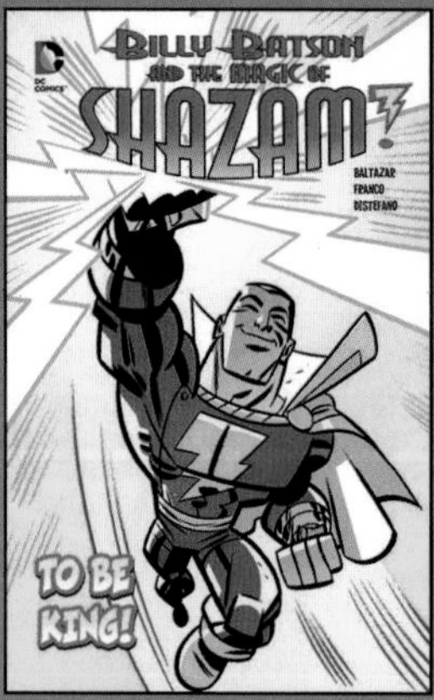
BILLY BATSON AND THE MAGIC OF SHAZAM!
BALTAZAR FRANCO DESTEFANO
TO BE KING!

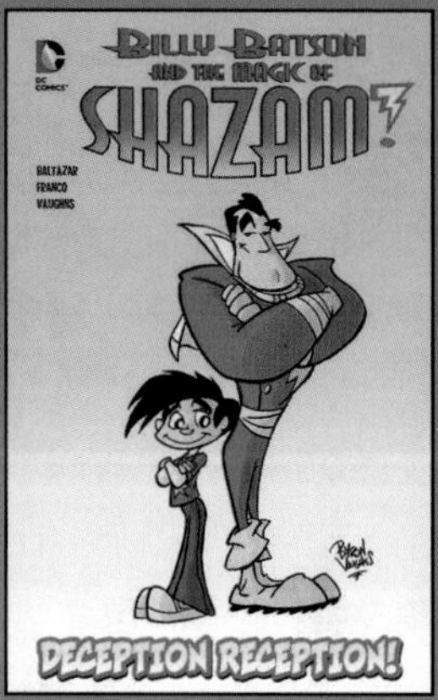
BILLY BATSON AND THE MAGIC OF SHAZAM!
BALTAZAR FRANCO VAUGHNS
DECEPTION RECEPTION!

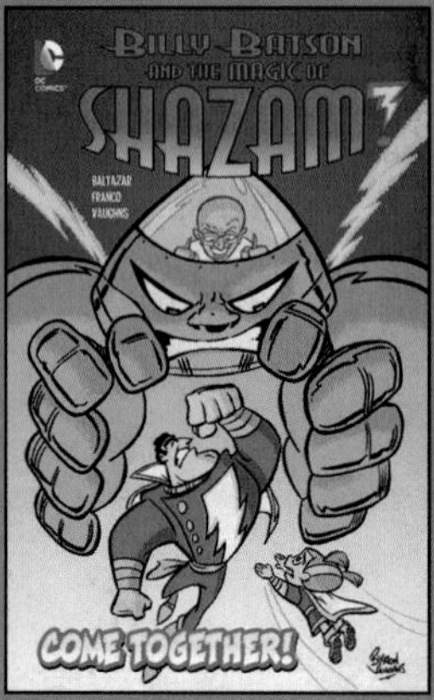
BILLY BATSON AND THE MAGIC OF SHAZAM!
BALTAZAR FRANCO VAUGHNS
COME TOGETHER!

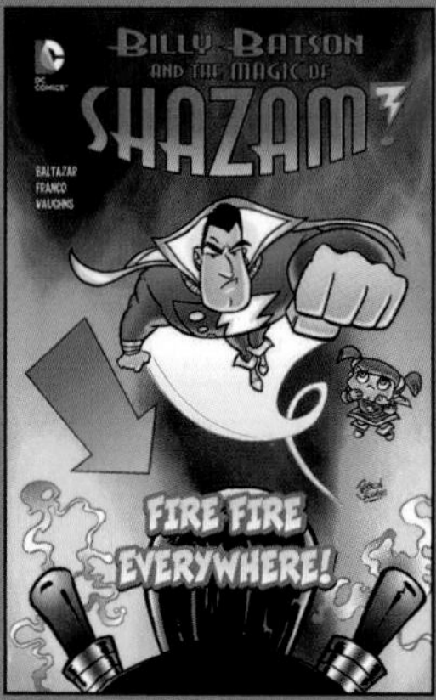
BILLY BATSON AND THE MAGIC OF SHAZAM!
BALTAZAR FRANCO VAUGHNS
FIRE FIRE EVERYWHERE!

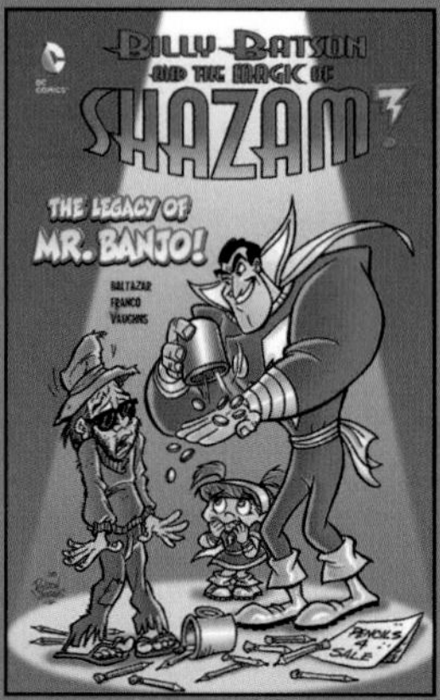
BILLY BATSON AND THE MAGIC OF SHAZAM!
THE LEGACY OF MR. BANJO!
BALTAZAR FRANCO VAUGHNS

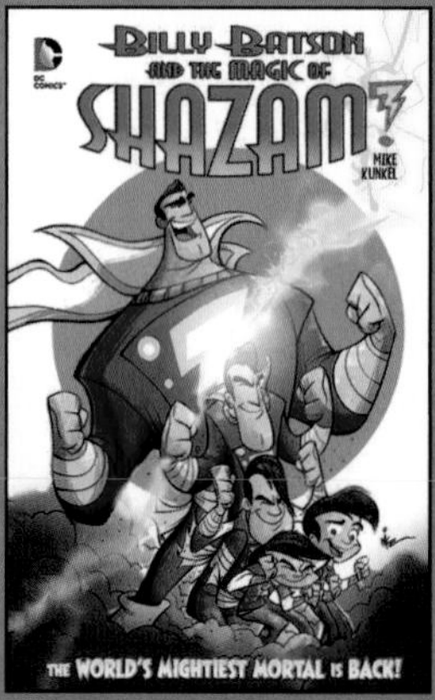
BILLY BATSON AND THE MAGIC OF SHAZAM!
MIKE KUNKEL
THE WORLD'S MIGHTIEST MORTAL IS BACK!

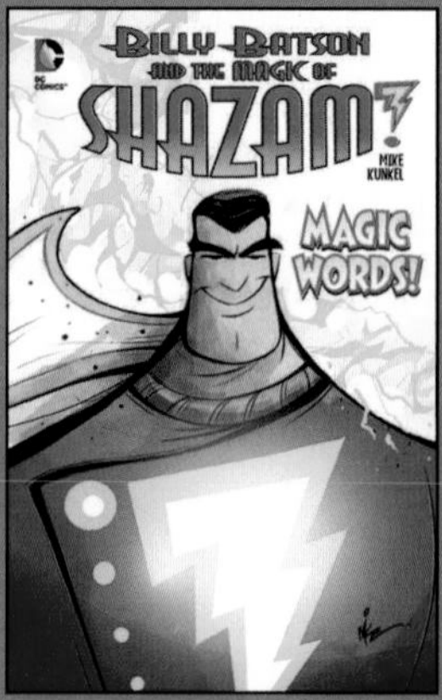
BILLY BATSON AND THE MAGIC OF SHAZAM!
MIKE KUNKEL
MAGIC WORDS!

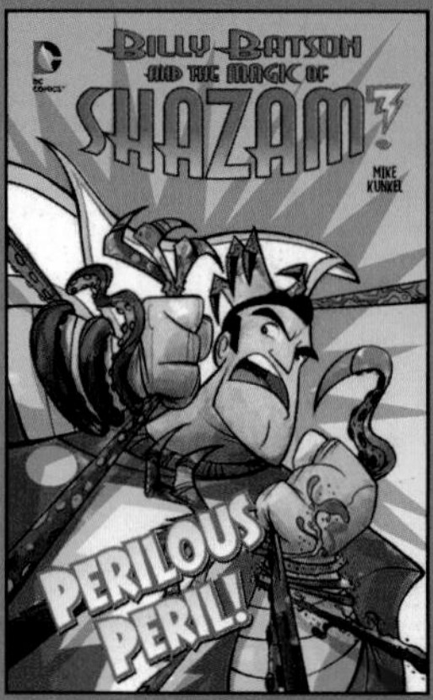
BILLY BATSON AND THE MAGIC OF SHAZAM!
MIKE KUNKEL
PERILOUS PERIL!

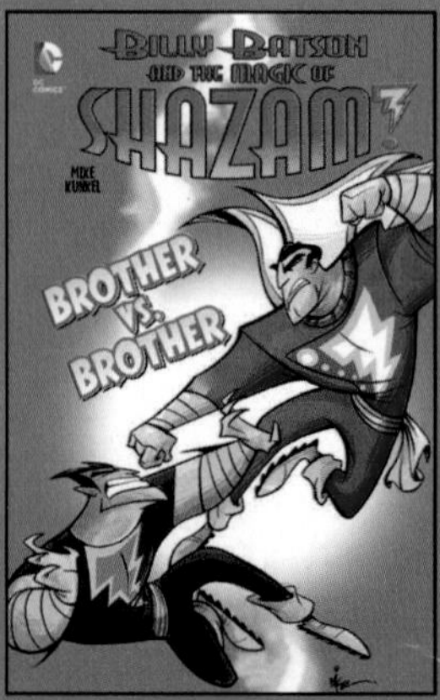
BILLY BATSON AND THE MAGIC OF SHAZAM!
MIKE KUNKEL
BROTHER VS. BROTHER